PUFFIN BOOKS

The Coconut Quins

Jan Mark grew up in Kent and attended the Canterbury College of Art. She went on to teach art in Gravesend. She started her writing career in 1974, and since then has written a large number of highly successful books, which have won numerous prestigious prizes including the Carnegie Medal. She spent two years as writer-in-residence at Oxford Polytechnic and now lives in Oxford.

D0268330

Some other books by Jan Mark

THE DEAD LETTER BOX
THE TWIG THING
THE SHORT VOYAGE OF THE *ALBERT ROSS*

For older readers

A FINE SUMMER KNIGHT
HAIRS IN THE PALM OF THE HAND
HANDLES
NOTHING TO BE AFRAID OF
THE SIGHTING
THUNDER AND LIGHTNINGS

In teenage fiction

FEET AND OTHER STORIES
THE HILLINGDON FOX

Jan Mark

THE
COCONUT
QUINS

Illustrated by Anna C. Leplar

PUFFIN BOOKS

PUFFIN BOOKS

Published by the Penguin Group
Penguin Books Ltd, 27 Wrights Lane, London W8 5TZ, England
Penguin Putnam Inc., 375 Hudson Street, New York,
New York 10014, USA
Penguin Books Australia Ltd, Ringwood, Victoria, Australia
Penguin Books Canada Ltd, 10 Alcorn Avenue, Toronto,
Ontario, Canada M4V 3B2
Penguin Books (NZ) Ltd, Cnr Rosedale and Airborne Roads, Albany,
Auckland, New Zealand

Penguin Books Ltd, Registered Offices: Harmondsworth,
Middlesex, England

First published by Viking 1997
Published in Puffin Books 1998
1 3 5 7 9 10 8 6 4 2

Text copyright © Jan Mark, 1997
Illustrations copyright © Anna C. Leplar, 1997
All rights reserved

The moral right of the author and illustrator has been asserted

Set in Palatino

Made and printed in England by Clays Ltd, St Ives plc

British Library Cataloguing in Publication Data
A CIP catalogue record for this book is available from
the British Library

ISBN 0–140–37859–6

This book is for Stoneydown Primary School

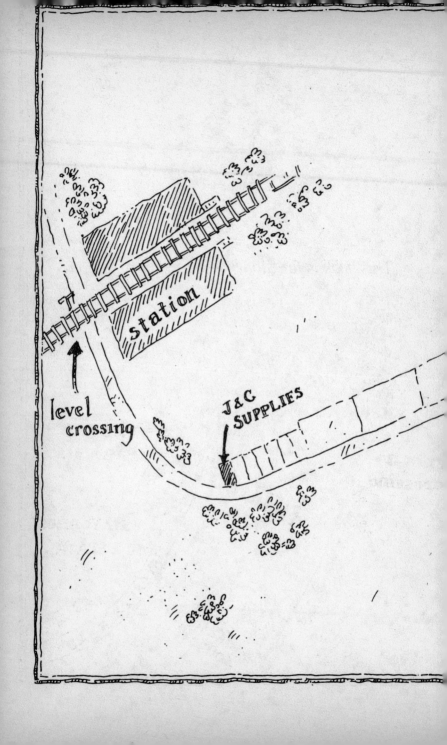

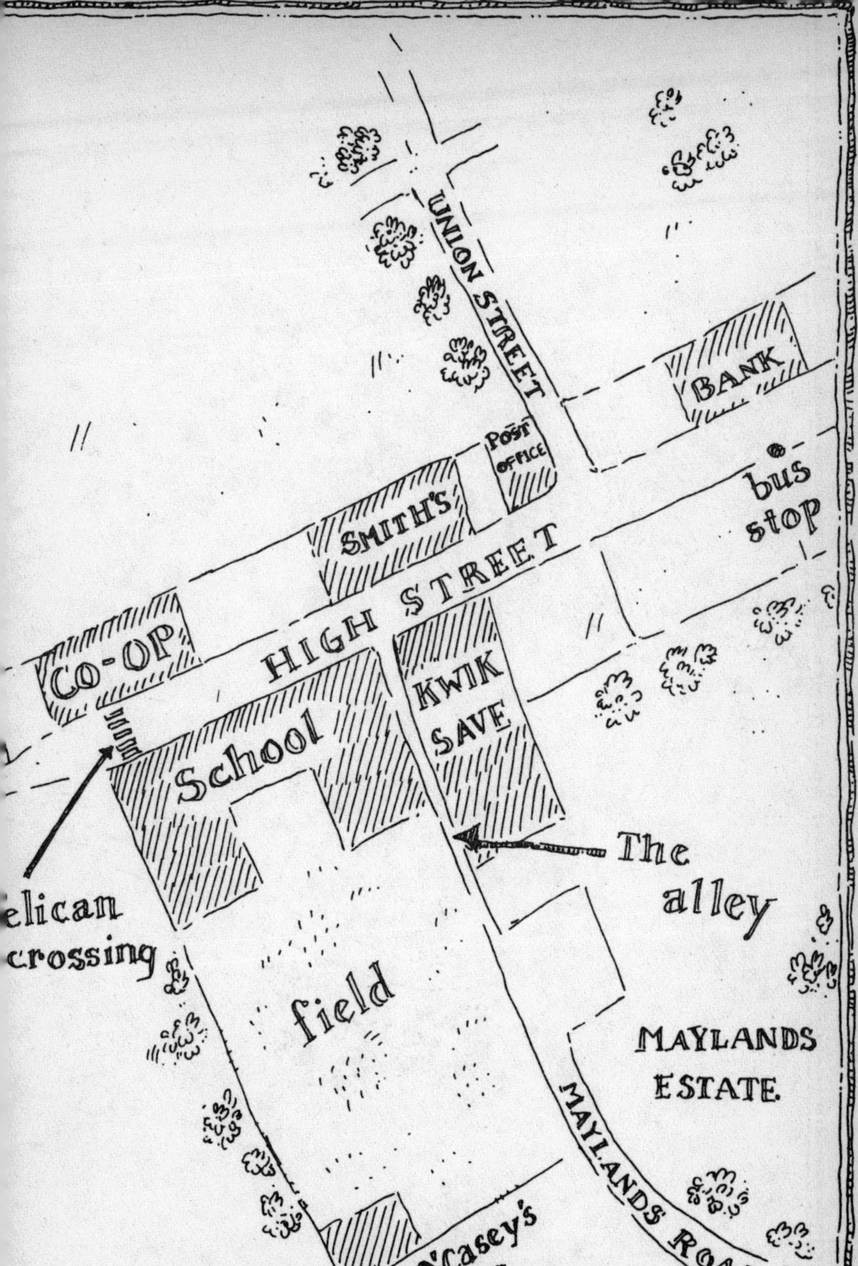

UNION STREET
BANK
POST OFFICE
bus stop
SMITH'S
HIGH STREET
CO-OP
KWIK SAVE
School
The alley
elican crossing
field
MAYLANDS ESTATE.
MAYLANDS ROAD
Mr O'Casey's house

One

Zena heard her mother talking about Paul
Chambers, in the Post Office.

"He looks like a coconut with that new
haircut."

"He had really pretty curls when he
was a baby," said Mrs Parker, behind the
counter. "More like a little girl."

Zena was not surprised that Paul
Chambers had turned out the way he
had. Nobody wanted to grow up hearing
that they had pretty girlie curls – even if
they were a girl.

Two days ago he had sneaked off to the
barber's with his uncle and come home
with a centimetre of bristles, like the back
door mat, and almost the same colour.
He was in Zena's class at school, so she
could not remember him as a baby, but in

any case, long before the haircut he had been busy proving how unlike a girl he was.

At the end of the alley by the school were two sets of metal bars, put there to stop people rushing out into the High Street and straight under a bus. Last term Paul and some friends had taken over the metal bars and lain in wait for those little kids who were not collected by grown-ups after school.

"This is a toll-gate," Paul informed them, "like on the Dartford Crossing and bridges and stuff. You have to pay a toll to get past," he explained to the little kids, who had not been in the lesson where Paul had learned about roads. "Tolls are money. If you can't pay you have to go the long way round."

"I'm not paying you nothing," said the biggest little kid, and tried to dodge under the bars. It might have been a game up to that moment, but then Paul and Stephen Shepherd jumped on the biggest little kid. There were thumps and punches and someone got kicked, and all the little kids, including the biggest, turned and ran back down the alley, crying and howling.

Nothing was said in assembly next day, but at home time Mr Grey, the head

teacher, strolled down the alley and caught the toll-gatherers red-handed.

That was the end of the toll-gate, but after this Paul and his friends hung around together in the playground and sneered dangerously when anyone came near them. They all wore boots instead of trainers and one by one they got the tough haircuts. Paul's mum, who could remember better than most what a pretty

baby Paul had been, held out the longest, but now here was Paul with the toughest haircut of all.

Just looking at it made you realize how hard his head must be.

Coconuts, Zena thought, looking at Paul's gang sitting round their table: Stephen Shepherd, Farroukh Hussein, Paul himself and the Redsell twins, Bruce and Dylan. They were not identical twins and had looked quite different, until the haircuts. Now all five looked exactly the same, sneering and scowling like –

"Miss, what's that you call five babies all born at the same time?" Zena said.

"Quintuplets – quins," Miss Barrett said, and looked where Zena was looking. "Mmmmm," said Miss Barrett.

After that Zena thought of Paul's gang as the Coconut Quins, but wisely did not tell them so. Teachers were always

moving the Quins to different tables, but
no one else much wanted to sit with them
and they always ended up back together
again.

After the latest move, Danny Carrick
found himself sitting at the Quins' table.
This was a bad mistake. Miss Barrett
would never have made it, but Miss
Barrett had left at Easter. Mrs Coles was
new – but old enough to know better,
Zena thought.

She glanced across the room to where Danny sat, looking sad and nervous under his fringe of soft dark hair, a spaniel among the coconuts. The Quins had already roughed him up for daring to sit at their table, even though it was not his fault.

Since the toll-gate incident there was always a teacher on duty in the alley, at home time, lurking near the metal bars. But not many people went home that

way. Nearly everyone at Maylands School lived on the Maylands Estate, including the Coconut Quins, and at half-past three they went streaming through the gate and turned right towards Maylands Road.

Danny Carrick was one of the few who turned left, slipped between the metal bars and vanished among the crowds in the High Street.

Today, Zena noticed, the Coconut Quins went after him, their boots clanking between the high brick walls on either side of the alley.

"Where are you lads off to?" said Mr Grey, who was on duty, manning the metal bars.

Paul immediately stuck out his jaw and clenched his fists as if Mr Grey had offered to fight him.

"Shopping for my nan."

"Oh yes?" Mr Grey leaned on the metal

bars in a friendly way, blocking the exit. "And what are you going to buy?"

Paul had his back to Zena but she saw his ears go red. He was obviously thinking fast.

"Cornflakes and that," he said. "Bread and stuff. Cat food." The ears turned crimson. "Carrots!"

"I hope you've got enough money," Mr Grey said.

"Loads," Paul said.

"Are you sure? I seem to remember having to lend you your swimming money this morning. Perhaps you had better go back to your nan's and get some more."

Mr Grey was quite thin but he seemed to have swelled to fill the gap between the bars.

With anyone else the Coconut Quins would have kicked their way through,

but not even Paul was going to risk kicking Mr Grey. The Quins turned, in a surly surge, and stomped back down the alley, jostling Zena, although there was plenty of room to pass.

"You don't go home this way, do you?" Mr Grey said, as Zena approached.

"I do now. We moved," Zena said.

"So you did." Mr Grey stepped aside politely to let her through.

Zena looked both ways along the street before heading for the pelican crossing, but by now there was no sign of Danny.

Two

Danny had not been at the school for very long and Zena had never wondered much about him, wondered where he came from, or where he lived.

And then, almost as soon as she began to wonder, she found out.

The alley by the school came out in the middle of the High Street, where the big shops were, the Co-op and Kwik Save, Boots and Smith's. To get to her new house, Zena had to cross the road and go down Union Street, next to the Post Office. She never went the other way, there was no need to. Mum's shopping began at the Post Office and ended at the Co-op, just beyond the pelican crossing. The only times that Zena ever saw the other end of the High Street were when they took the bus to Gran's, every other Saturday.

They were going there this Saturday, catching the bus at the stop opposite the bank. Usually the bus was a small one, but today it was a double-decker.

"Can we go upstairs?" Zena said. Except for the visits to Gran they hardly ever went anywhere by bus, and usually there was no upstairs to go on.

"With this lot?" Mum said. She was holding Kyle under one arm and folding the buggy with the other hand. Zena had Rose on reins, held tight, near the harness, because Rose knew just how to wind herself round the bus stop.

"Well, can *I* go upstairs?"

"All right." They were scrambling aboard and Zena had to hold Kyle as well, while Mum stowed the buggy in the cave under the stairs. It seemed to have

been made specially so that buggies
would not fit into it. "But if Rose starts
to act up you'll have to come down
again."

"How will I know?"

"You'll hear, won't you?" Rose's acting
up was famous and very loud.

There was only one other person
upstairs, sitting near the back. Zena went
to the front and sat staring ahead,

wondering how it was that the bus seemed to be so much wider than the road. It looked as if it must knock down street lamps and rip off shop signs as it roared along the High Street, leaving a trail of destruction, like a tornado.

She saw the pelican crossing and remembered to look down the alley. After that they were in foreign territory. On the little buses you saw just what you could see from the pavement, only slightly higher up. From the top of this bus you could see into upstairs windows. The windows over the big shops were mostly blanked out, but once past the pelican crossing the High Street got narrower, and Zena noticed that here the buildings were only shops downstairs. The upstairs parts had people living in them, they were flats. She could have seen right into the windows, only most of them had lace curtains – because of people like her.

Near to the station the bus slowed down beside the strangest row of shops she had seen, although she realized that they would not look strange if she were standing on the pavement. The shops had been built out in front of houses, real houses with sloping roofs and chimney pots. The shops themselves had flat roofs, and these roofs had become little front

gardens for the houses. There were fences round them, and plant pots, washing lines, toys. There was even a swing in one.

Now the bus was stuck because round the corner the gates had closed on the level crossing. Zena leaned forward in her

seat and looked down. These shops were not like Smith's and the Co-op. They were small, each with just one window and one doorway. Dawson Newsagent and Tobacconist; The Jolly Cobbler, Shoe Repairs; Starlite Snack Bar; a dry cleaner's; Katrina, Ladies' Hairdresser and a betting

shop. The last one in the row had a sign over the window saying J & C Supplies.

Although Zena passed them every fortnight on the bus, she had never bothered to look at them before because they seemed so dull. Now she peered down, trying to see what it was that J & C supplied. It was difficult to look in at the window from that angle, but it seemed to be full of dark green and brown things; clothes, boxes, folded blankets. There was a cluster of tin buckets hanging up and a stack of metal basins, all in the same drab colours. Who would want to buy supplies like that?

Zena looked at the flat above the shop. The bus was moving again now, but it was still going slowly enough for her to see that the flat roof that lay like a lid over J & C Supplies was a proper garden with tubs of flowers, patio chairs, and gnomes with fishing rods, standing round a rockery. There was even a window box, full of geraniums.

The last thing Zena saw, as the bus turned the corner, was Danny Carrick, looking out of the window between the geraniums.

A hooting howl echoed in the stairway. Rose was acting up. Zena went down to

hold Kyle on her lap while Mum saw to Rose. Rose was not ill or unhappy, just bored. She got bored very easily unless someone was looking at her. Now everyone on the bottom deck was looking at her, and Rose was jumping up and down on the seat, to celebrate.

Zena took Kyle and Mum grabbed the reins and began to reel Rose in. When Rose had been plugged with a lolly, Zena said, "Mum, what's J & C Supplies?"

"Who are they when they're washed?" Mum said.

"That shop back there, near the station. By the betting shop."

"How should I know?"

"It's got buckets and things in the window."

"Then it's probably a bucket shop."

"Someone from school lives upstairs of it," Zena said. "Danny Carrick."

"Then Danny Carrick's probably got more buckets than he's had hot dinners," Mum said. "Lucky old Danny."

But Zena knew that there were other things in the window besides buckets. Who would have thought that Danny's family owned a shop?

Three

On Sunday morning Zena took a walk along the High Street. Mum thought that she was going to the estate to play with Manda Richards who had once lived next door.

"I still live next door," Manda said. "It was you that moved."

I'll go to the estate later, Zena thought, to make it true, and looked down the alley past the metal bars.

It took only a few minutes to reach the row of shops where Danny lived. Today they were closed. The tables were empty in the snack bar. Katrina's hair driers nodded in the shadows like the heads of drowsy giants and The Jolly Cobbler was dark and sinister, not at all jolly.

Dawson Newsagent and Tobacconist

was open, but J & C Supplies had a metal shutter drawn down in front, like an enormous fireguard, barring the window and doorway. The supplies must be very valuable, thought Zena. At the other end of the High Street only jewellers and video shops had shutters like that.

Zena peered through the grille. There were the buckets, coils of rope, tin cans with handles, long metal boxes, all painted those dull colours that made her think of soldiers. A row of black boots stood to attention behind the glass and above them hung a bundle of bootlaces, as long as skipping-ropes. The back of the window was lined with dirty yellow pegboard and from it hung sweaters, trousers, belts; green, green, more green, green and brown, like camouflage.

It *was* camouflage. And the things that she had thought must be basins were

helmets. Zena looked at the boots. Was
this where soldiers did their shopping?
Did they come here to buy their guns as
well? No wonder there was a shutter in
front.

Something told her that it was not very
likely that a soldier would go out with
a shopping bag for a packet of bullets,
economy-size, and a kilo of hand-
grenades. Anyway, there were no soldiers
in town. But there must be something in

J & C Supplies that was not shown in the window. Surely no one would break in to steal buckets and bootlaces.

Zena looked up at the sign over the shop. The pavement was so narrow that she could not step back far enough to see what stood above it, so she crossed the road.

From there she could see the railings that fenced off Danny's front garden, and beyond them the top of Danny's house.

The windows were shut and there seemed to be no one at home, but she waved in case Danny might be looking out. In the next garden, above the betting shop, a man was watering plants in a tub, and over the hairdresser's was a washing line where fifteen identical blue towels hung in a row.

She counted them. They must belong to Katrina. How nice it must be to own a shop, and live on top of it, so that you could go home whenever you felt like it.

Zena walked back to the alley and went to see Manda Richards, who lived in Maylands Road, just past the school.

On the school field, where they were not supposed to be, the Coconut Quins were leaping around, kicking each other, doing the unarmed combat that they had learned from watching cartoons on the telly. At least, for once, they were not

kicking anyone else. Zena supposed that they were getting ready for playtime, tomorrow morning. She wondered if they would be so nasty to Danny if they knew that he owned an Army shop; or rather, that his mum and dad did.

From the house at the end of the field Mr O'Casey the caretaker was striding towards the Quins. Mr O'Casey was always bearing down on people who were doing things he thought they ought not to be doing. People with any sense stopped at once and walked quietly away, but the Quins went on leaping about, kicking the air and chopping at nothing with their hands. From a distance they did not look at all threatening. They looked like the Thunderbirds puppets with their strings in a twist.

Zena could hear Mr O'Casey shouting, but the Quins let him come right up to

them before they started to leave the field.
They went very slowly, still kicking and
chopping, and Zena did not wait until
they reached the gate. It was padlocked,
she noticed as she went by. The Quins
must have climbed over it.

When she got to Manda's house she
began to wish that she had not bothered
to come. Manda was having a Sindy doll
wedding on the doorstep. The
bridegroom was another Sindy doll with

its hair cut short and a felt-tip beard. They were sitting on the doorstep when the Quins went past.

"Your dad at home?" Paul said, when he saw them.

"No," Manda said, before Zena could tell her to take no notice. Paul behaved himself when people's dads were about. Paul put on his sneer, like a false moustache, and unlatched the gate. Manda dropped the Sindy bride and ran up the path.

"You can't come in here."

"Who said I was coming in?" Paul and Farroukh began to swing the gate open and shut.

"Get off of our gate."

"It's not your gate, it belongs to the council. So does the wall." Bruce and Dylan Redsell immediately climbed on to the wall. It was only half a metre high and

Manda's mum had planted lavender bushes beside it. Bruce and Dylan began swiping at the lavender sprigs with sticks.

Manda tried to hold the gate shut, but Paul and Farroukh had discovered that if you banged it shut hard enough the latch slipped and it bounced open again. Stephen Shepherd climbed on to the gate and rode backwards and forwards as it swung.

Manda was starting to cry. "I'll tell my mum."

"She can't do nothing," Dylan Redsell said, smashing at the bushes with his stick.

"If your mum says anything to us there won't be any bushes by tomorrow night," Paul said, casually.

"We'll tell the police."

"Tell them what?"

"That you pulled up our bushes."

"I never said that, did I?" He looked at the others and they all sneered. "I just said there wouldn't be any bushes. Know what I mean?"

The five of them swaggered away, down the street, kicking at car wheels and gates and fences, buzzing stones, booting a cola can along the gutter.

"Don't take any notice," Zena said, as Manda, crying properly now, trailed back to the doorstep. But it was too late for that.

Four

On Monday morning the Coconut Quins got ready for Danny by moving his chair from their table and squeezing it in among the six at Zena's table.

"You can sit with us," Zena said, but that was not allowed, unless someone else moved to the Quins' table. No one would.

Danny was still standing when Mrs Coles came out of the stock cupboard.

"Sit down, Danny."

"My chair's gone, Miss," Danny said. "Someone moved it."

"Well, move it back."

"Can't I sit on it where it is?"

Mrs Coles looked at where it was. "Of course not, there's no room. Put it back and sit down and don't make such a fuss."

Danny fetched his chair and sat down.

"Thought we told you not to sit here," Bruce Redsell said quietly, and he smiled when he said it so that Mrs Coles would think that he was being nice.

At break the Quins barged out first to kick themselves round the playground. They would have been kicking Danny, but Zena called him over to share her crisps.

"That's right, hide with the girlies," Farroukh yelled, and the Quins all sneered together.

"Don't take any notice," Manda said. She had learned something since yesterday.

"I know where you live," Zena said to Danny. "I saw you on the bus on Saturday."

"I wasn't on the bus on Saturday," Danny said.

"No, *I* was on the bus. You were looking out of the window, over that shop."

"What shop?" Manda said. "I never knew you had a shop."

"J & C Supplies," Zena said, as Danny's mouth was full of crisps. "It's an Army shop."

Danny butted in, blowing out crisps like shrapnel. "Ex-Army."

"What d'you mean, ex-Army?"

"Things the Army doesn't use any more."

"What, like those boots?"

They had not noticed that the Quins had gone once round the playground and were now standing behind Danny.

"Does it sell knives?" Paul Chambers said.

Danny turned round, expecting to be

thumped, but Paul was looking almost friendly.

"Yes, shelves and shelves of them."

"And Ninja thingies?" Stephen Shepherd said.

"Army don't use Ninja thingies," Paul said. "Shuddup, Shepherd."

Stephen sneered a bit but not too much, because it was Paul who had told him to shut up.

"What shop are you on about?" Farroukh said.

"J & C," Danny said. "We live over the top of it."

For once in his life Paul did not sneer.

"J & C Supplies down near the station? That's your shop?"

"Yes," Zena said, before Danny could answer. "Well, his mum and dad's."

"You own J & C?" Paul looked even more surprised.

Danny swallowed the last of his crisps and nodded vigorously.

"Can you get stuff out of it? Have they got guns and stuff? I seen those ammo boxes in the window. Do you sell ammunition? They got bayonets?"

All the Quins were talking at once, and suddenly Zena and Manda found themselves standing alone. Danny had gone, and was stomping round the

playground. There were six Quins now,
instead of five.

"What did you tell them that for?"
Manda said. "Why'd you tell them it was
his shop?"

"It *is* his shop. I saw him at the window,
upstairs."

"My Auntie Esther lives over a shop,"
Manda said. "It's the Woolwich Building
Society. If my Auntie Esther owned the

Woolwich Building Society we'd be rich, wouldn't we?"

"But the hairdresser lives over her shop. I saw the towels on the line."

"Well, maybe it is his shop then," Manda said. "But you needn't have told them."

"I thought they might leave him alone." That was the truth. When she had said it Zena had thought that perhaps the Quins would give Danny a bit of respect if they knew that Danny's family owned J & C Supplies.

"They haven't though, have they?"

Zena looked at the six Quins in the distance. "No," she said, at last.

But they were certainly giving Danny a bit of respect.

When the whistle went at the end of break, Zena went in behind Danny.

"I didn't mean to say anything. Is it really your shop?"

"Yeah, 'course it is." Danny seemed to have got bigger in the last ten minutes.

He sat down at the Quins' table quite happily, and slouched like the others, with his feet stuck out, tripping people up.

When Mrs Coles came in everyone sat up straight, ready to start work.

"All got your pencils?" Mrs Coles said.

Danny slid even further down in his seat and picked up his pencil. It was a new yellow one with a good sharp point. He looked at the Quins, he looked at Mrs Coles, took the pencil in both hands and snapped it in two.

"Yeah," said Danny, toughly. "I got my pencil."

Zena heard the crack. It seemed that more than the pencil had broken.

Five

At home time the Quins turned down the alley instead of right, up Maylands Road.

"Shopping for your nan again, Paul?" asked Mr Grey, at the metal bars.

"Nah, we're going round Danny's," Paul said.

"Is that right, Danny?" Mr Grey sounded surprised.

"Yeah, I asked 'em," Danny said, out of the side of his mouth.

Zena followed at a safe distance and stayed on her side of the road when the others went over the pelican crossing. The Quins walked in a bunch, bumping into people on purpose. They did their synchronized sneering when anyone told them to watch where they were going.

When they reached the doorway of
J & C Supplies they leaned in a row
against the window, as if they all owned
the shop.

Next morning Danny went into the
cloakroom and put water on his hair.
When he came out again he had slicked it
straight back from his forehead so that his
skull looked small and hard, like the
others. Then he went into the classroom

and threw bits of paper about in a
menacing way.

"I'm surprised at you, Danny," Mrs
Coles said when she came in. "Pick it all
up at once."

"Yeah, I might," Danny said, and
picked up the bits of paper very slowly.
He managed to knock over two chairs, a
tub of crayons and the class begonia
while he was doing it.

"I don't know what's got into you," Mrs Coles said, several times during the day.

Zena said nothing. She knew what had got into Danny and she had a nasty feeling that she had put it there.

When it was time to wash up the painting things at the end of the afternoon, she found herself next to Danny at the sink.

"Get out of the way," Danny said, and spilled paint water on her shoes.

"What do you want to be like them for?" Zena said. "They only let you go with them because of the shop."

"They're my friends," Danny said.

"He's going to get us weapons," Stephen Shepherd said. "Nobody won't give us any trouble, then."

"It's against the law to carry knives," Manda said.

"Oh dear. She's worried about her

mummy's flowers," Farroukh said, shoving through to the sink with a bunch of dripping paintbrushes. Even a paintbrush could look dangerous in Farroukh's hands. "Who said anything about knives?"

"You said weapons."

"Yeah, well, there's all sorts of weapons, aren't there?" Dylan Redsell said.

"I suppose he's going to get you a tank," Zena said.

Danny squared up to her. "Just watch it, right?"

As the week went on, Danny got tougher. He was sent off in rounders. He and the Quins shoved and stamped around, bragging about the weapons that Danny was going to get from J & C Supplies.

"Yeah, well, I can't just walk in and take them," Danny said. "I can't just *get* them.

I'll have to ask my dad. He's away at the moment."

That was on Wednesday.

By Friday Paul had a better plan. "We'll all go in together and some of us can talk to the selling person and Danny can get the weapons and do a runner."

"They're all in glass cases," Danny said. "With big locks on." Zena thought he sounded worried.

"Well, can't you go downstairs during the night and get them?" Stephen Shepherd said.

"You can't get into the shop from ours," Danny said. "Not inside."

"When's your dad coming back?" Bruce Redsell said.

"Next week," Danny said.

Zena was becoming more and more certain that Danny's mum and dad did

not own J & C Supplies. Danny said that C stood for Carrick and J stood for Mr Jones who had died, but she did not believe him. If only she had said nothing. If only Danny had admitted it was not true. Danny might be one of the Quins at the moment, while they thought they could get something out of him, but what was going to happen when days turned into weeks and weeks into months, and still they had no weapons?

Meanwhile they all drew tattoos on their arms with blue biro, daggers and snakes and skulls, and wrote threatening words on their knuckles, which no one could read because none of them could spell.

"When's your dad coming back?" Farroukh wanted to know, on Tuesday morning.

"Dunno," Danny muttered. "Soon . . ."

Danny had never mentioned his dad until Zena said that he owned the shop. Perhaps he did not have a dad. She felt worse and worse.

"Now don't do anything silly and come to school on Monday," Mrs Coles said, on Friday afternoon. It was just as well that she did say it. Zena had forgotten that half-term was coming.

"We'll be round yours on Monday, eh?" Paul said to Danny.

"We're going away for half-term," Danny said. He looked relieved.

"We'll come round anyway," Dylan said, and all the Quins looked at each other and laughed.

"I expect the shop will be open, though."

"Wonder if you can get in round the back."

"Wonder if you can *break* in round the back . . ."

Zena wanted to talk to Danny alone,
but Danny never was alone, these days.

Still, at home time she followed the six
Quins down the alley and over the
pelican crossing. Mingling with the
crowds, like a detective following a
suspect, she walked behind them to the
shop. But they went straight past, turned
along a path down the side of J & C
Supplies and disappeared.

Zena waited a few moments and then
went down the path too. It ran straight
beside a high fence and then turned
again, to run along the backs of the shops.
There were iron staircases going up to the
flats, like fire escapes, and on the first
staircase the Quins were sitting. Danny
was on the bottom step and the others
would not let him go any higher.

She turned and went back again before

anyone saw her. On the way past J & C Supplies she paused and looked in. The boots were still there in a row at the front of the window, but the rest of the window was empty, except for the bunch of bootlaces, hanging like dreadlocks. The door was open; she could see right inside to where the weapons were kept, but she could not see any weapons. There did not seem to be anything at all in J & C Supplies except for a bare counter and an empty cupboard, and one dangling light bulb, without a shade.

Six

On Saturday the bus to Gran's was a single-decker again. Zena knew that she would not be able to see Danny's house and garden, but she looked out at J & C Supplies.

The crossing gates were open today so the bus went by quite quickly, but not so quickly that she could not see that now the window was completely empty. Even the boots had marched away. There was a big poster pasted to the glass, but no time to see what was printed on it.

Because of the one-way system the bus did not pass the shops coming home again, but later that evening, sent out to buy milk, Zena scooted along the High Street to see what had happened.

A lot had happened. The poster said:

Moving to bigger premises
from 1 June J & C Supplies
will be at 15 Castle Street

Behind the poster the pegboard had
been taken down and she could see right
into the shop. It was full of planks and
boxes and paint cans. The helmets had
gone, the ammunition boxes had gone,
and the camouflage clothes, the buckets
and blankets and bootlaces. J & C,
whoever they were, had left, taking their
supplies with them.

Zena ran down the path to the back of
the shops, clambered up the first iron
staircase and banged on the door that was
Danny's.

But Danny and his family had already
gone, too.

Every day, through half-term, Zena

went along to the shop, and every day it
changed. Once it had been dark and
mysterious inside, Army green outside.
Now it was pink, with white shelves
along each wall. The paint round the
windows turned from green to white, and
the door was bright yellow.

On Friday she saw a man on a ladder
painting over the words J & C Supplies,

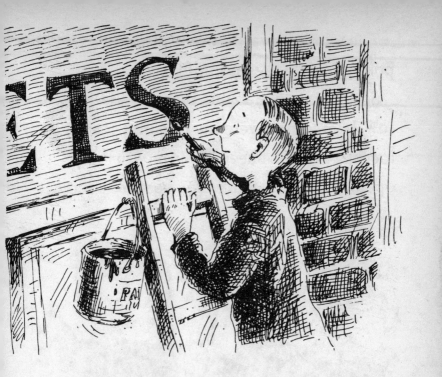

and on Saturday there was a new name
above the door: Moppets.

Zena looked in at the window. A pink
carpet lay on the floor. The white shelves
were stacked with little lacy woolly
clothes, and two pretty girls were
arranging baby frocks on tiny coathangers
along a rail down the middle, between a
row of prams and a row of cradles.

The window was full of rattles and potties, soft quilts and fluffy toys.

Something made Zena turn round. In a row, behind her, were the Coconut Quins, too surprised to sneer. Their mouths were open, which was a mistake, because Bruce

and Dylan still had some milk teeth which made them look harmless.

Zena did not stay to hear what they thought, she went over to see Manda Richards, whose Sindy doll was having a baby. But she did wonder what the Quins were going to say to Danny when he came back on Monday.

On Monday the Quins had nothing to say to Danny. They said it to everyone else.

"Baby clothes, baby clothes!" they chanted. "Danny Moppet's fluffy bunnies! How much is that potty in the window?"

Danny sat at the table looking smaller and smaller. His hair dried out and flopped forwards into a fringe again. At home time the Quins followed him down the alley, stamping their boots in time to the chanting.

"Baby clothes! Baby clothes! Dis-pos-able *nappies*!"

They were at it again on Tuesday. But at home time, as they were crossing the playground to the gate, Zena saw a huge man standing by the fence. He too had a coconut haircut, but no sneer, so he just looked tidy, not violent.

"You must be Danny's friends," said the huge man. "Well, pleased to meet you. I'm Danny's dad."

The Quins stopped chanting and pulled up so suddenly that they all ran into each other. Danny went to stand behind his dad. Zena thought of King Kong.

"You seem to be giving our Danny a hard time," said his dad. "What's the problem?"

No one said anything. Then Paul stepped forward.

"He *lied*," said Paul, as though such a terrible thing had never happened before. "He said you owned the Army shop and

now it's selling baby clothes and potties
and prams."

"He said he'd get us weapons,"
Farroukh muttered.

"I didn't," Danny whispered. "*You* said
that. I never."

"If I wanted to sell baby clothes I
would," said Danny's huge dad. "But I
wouldn't sell weapons because if I did I'd

have to deal with people like you. I've
had enough of weapons. I was in the
Army ten years. Now I do sell things. I
sell flowers, off a barrow down the
station. Want to make something of it?"

Very slowly the Quins were backing
away, not a sneer in sight.

"My wife says you hang around our
place. I don't want to see any of you

hanging around our place again. Get it?
Not unless you make proper friends with
our Dan. Got it?"

The Quins had got it. They went
through the gate and turned right, up
Maylands Road. Danny crept out from
behind his dad and took his hand.

"You aren't one of them, are you?"
Danny's dad said, when he saw Zena.

"Danny didn't mean to lie," Zena said.
"It was my fault. I thought you owned
J & C."

"He didn't have to let them think you
were right, did he?" Danny's dad said.
"He didn't want to let on I sold flowers."
He gave Danny a friendly shake, and then
he said, "Ha! Baby clothes! Moppets! Best
thing that could have happened."

He roared with laughter. He really did
roar and Mr O'Casey came out to see
what was going on.

Zena thought of what someone like King Kong could do with a coconut, and decided that the Quins had got off very lightly indeed.

Also in Young Puffin

The
<u>Twig</u> <u>Thing</u>

Jan Mark

As soon as Rosie and Ella saw the house they knew that something was missing.

It has lots of windows and stairs, but where is the garden? After they move in, Rosie finds a twig thing which she puts in water on the window-sill. Gradually things begin to change.

READ MORE IN PUFFIN

For children of all ages, Puffin represents quality and variety – the very best in publishing today around the world.

For complete information about books available from Puffin – and Penguin – and how to order them, contact us at the appropriate address below. Please note that for copyright reasons the selection of books varies from country to country.

On the worldwide web: www.puffin.co.uk

In the United Kingdom: Please write to *Dept. EP, Penguin Books Ltd, Bath Road, Harmondsworth, West Drayton, Middlesex UB7 ODA*

In the United States: Please write to *Consumer Sales, Penguin USA, P.O. Box 999, Dept. 17109, Bergenfield, New Jersey 07621-0120.* VISA and MasterCard holders call 1-800-253-6476 to order Penguin titles

In Canada: Please write to *Penguin Books Canada Ltd, 10 Alcorn Avenue, Suite 300, Toronto, Ontario M4V 3B2*

In Australia: Please write to *Penguin Books Australia Ltd, P.O. Box 257, Ringwood, Victoria 3134*

In New Zealand: Please write to *Penguin Books (NZ) Ltd, Private Bag 102902, North Shore Mail Centre, Auckland 10*

In India: Please write to *Penguin Books India Pvt Ltd, 706 Eros Apartments, 56 Nehru Place, New Delhi 110 019*

In the Netherlands: Please write to *Penguin Books Netherlands bv, Postbus 3507, NL-1001 AH Amsterdam*

In Germany: Please write to *Penguin Books Deutschland GmbH, Metzlerstrasse 26, 60594 Frankfurt am Main*

In Spain: Please write to *Penguin Books S. A., Bravo Murillo 19, 1° B, 28015 Madrid*

In Italy: Please write to *Penguin Italia s.r.l., Via Felice Casati 20, I 20124 Milano.*

In France: Please write to *Penguin France S. A., 17 rue Lejeune, F–31000 Toulouse*

In Japan: Please write to *Penguin Books Japan, Ishikiribashi Building, 2–5–4, Suido, Bunkyo-ku, Tokyo 112*

In South Africa: Please write to *Longman Penguin Southern Africa (Pty) Ltd, Private Bag X08, Bertsham 2013*